By Don M. Winn
Illustrated by Dave Allred

*This book is dedicated to my dad, the greatest hero of my youth,
who was always there when I needed him the most.*

How to use this book:

Cardboard Box Adventures books are books worth talking about. They are designed to give parents and children an opportunity to have meaningful discussions about important topics. The stories are just the beginning. Please read them aloud with your children and then use the questions included at the end of the stories to begin conversations with them. Many of the questions will help you to see how well your child understood the story. Others will help you and your children talk about what's on their minds and what's important to them, drawing you closer together and strengthening the loving bond you already share.

All Cardboard Box Adventures books are available in hardcover, softcover and eBook formats. Take them to the next level with interactive versions from InteractBooks™ (www.interactbooks.com).

Superhero
ISBN: 978-0-88144-514-5
Copyright © 2010 by Don M. Winn

Published by Cardboard Box Adventures
www.donwinn.com

Introduction:

What is a hero? In comic books and movies, heroes sometimes have some kind of amazing power that they use to help other people. But real heroes are ordinary people that do ordinary things to help others. If you can find a way to help someone who really needs your help, you will always be a hero to that person.

Most of the time, the ordinary people doing ordinary things to help us are the most important people in our lives. With this idea of a hero in mind, I can't think of a greater hero than a loving parent.

I give you Superhero!

It was just another average day,
I hadn't time for school or play,
a hero's call I must obey,
a Superhero, I!

With super ears I hear the call,
there's panic at the city mall,
it's up to me to save them all,
a Superhero, I!

At fighting crime I am an ace,
I wear a mask to hide my face,
with super speed I'm on the case,
a Superhero, I!

With my super strength and x-ray eyes,
all crooks will soon meet their demise,
it matters not a hero's size,
a Superhero, I!

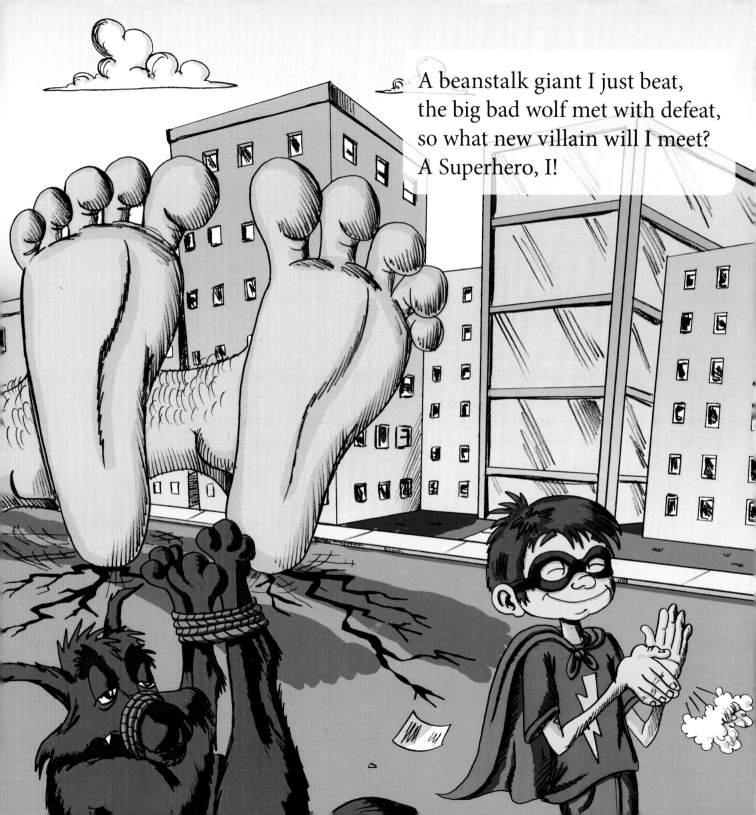

Stopped in my tracks at Tenth and Green,
where frightened crowds ran from the scene,
I wondered what this sight could mean,
a Superhero, I!

While waiting for the smoke to clear,
two villains just ahead appear,
unwanted DREAD and evil FEAR!
A Superhero, I!

Before the villains I could scold,
DREAD quickly turned my body cold,
as FEAR confined me in its hold,
a Superhero, I!

They're not like any other foe,
they have a red and orange glow,
the more I'm scared, the more they grow,
a Superhero, I!

Each step I tried to make was slow,
I couldn't stay, but couldn't go,
my super strength now ceased to flow,
a Superhero, I!

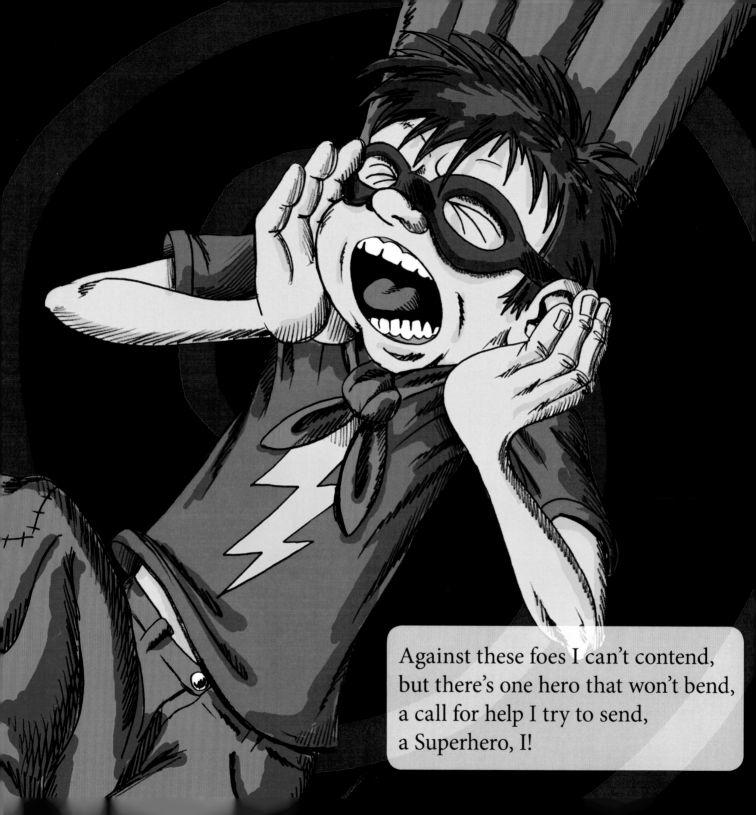

Against these foes I can't contend,
but there's one hero that won't bend,
a call for help I try to send,
a Superhero, I!

Just then I woke upon my bed,
my dad was standing overhead,
then FEAR soon left as well as DREAD,
a Superhero, I!

For in defeat I will not fall,
when there's a hero I can call,
the greatest hero of them all,
it is my dad, not I!

QUESTIONS PARENTS CAN DISCUSS WITH THEIR CHILDREN

1. What is a hero?

2. Do you need to have super powers to be a hero?

3. How was the dad in this story a hero to his son?

4. How could you be a hero?

5. Who is your greatest hero and why?

CPSIA information can be obtained
at www.ICGtesting.com
Printed in the USA
393516LV00006B/46